BEACH BAGS

MICHAEL KINGSWOOD

ISBN 13: 978-1-950683-16-1

ISBN 10: 1-950683-16-8

 Created with Vellum

Contents

About This Book

An abandoned bag, filled with money and with what appears to be a bloody handprint on the side, upends Harry's relaxing day at the beach.

Beach Bags is a 5,000 word short mystery.

Enjoy the book! After you're done, please come to Michael's website and sign up for his mailing list at michaelkingswood.com/newsletter-signup/. Guaranteed to be spam free, he uses it to announce new releases and special promotions for his fans.

Beach Bags

A light-brown leather handbag doesn't normally just hang out on the beach by itself, but for some reason this one was. No one's blanket or umbrella lay within a hundred feet of it. In fact, except for the little indentation the bag left, the sand appeared to have not been disturbed at all for almost that same area around it.

Harry had just decided he had enough of sweltering on the sand for one day, and that it was time for a cool swim. He packed, donned his navy blue Ron Jon tank top, folded up his beach chair, and was tramping back toward the narrow path that cut through the dunes to the street his vacation rental lay on when he spied it. Normally he wouldn't really have cared to notice, but the strangeness of a bag like that, more a valise than the sort of bag a person would bring to the beach, drew his eye. He slowed and came to a stop, squinting at it from behind the dark lenses of his shades, and frowned.

He turned to the closest people to him, a plump and sunburning couple in their mid-50s who clearly were from somewhere north, and cooler, and raised his voice to carry to them. "Hey, you know whose bag that is?"

The woman, in a one-piece multicolored swimsuit, raised her head from where she had been dozing in her reclining chair, looked toward the bag Harry was pointing at, and shrugged. "Haven't seen anyone near it all morning."

"Was it there when you got here?"

The woman traded looks with her husband, but also shrugged. "Not sure." She paused, looking back at Harry for a second as though waiting for another question. When he didn't immediately follow up, she sank back into her chair and let her head loll back comfortably again.

Harry rolled his eyes. Tourists.

Frowning, he turned back to the bag and pondered it for a few seconds. It really was none of his business. Hell, the owner would probably be back for it any minute now. And the pool was calling out sweetly to him. That, and a cold beer. He almost turned away, but then he noticed something else - a darker patch on the side of the bag, reddish, and shaped like...

It was a handprint. What the hell?

Harry dropped his beach bag and the folding chair, then hurried over to where the bag lay in the sand. He squatted down and looked more closely at it, and at the handprint. It was definitely reddish, and glistened slightly in the light of the noonday sun. Suddenly, he no longer felt the heat of the muggy July day; the chill going up his spine more than washed it away.

Licking his lips with a tongue that had suddenly gone dry, he reached out one finger and touched the handprint. It was wet, sticky, and the fingertip came away red.

He should have run away right then. Run away

and called the cops. Because seriously, a bag with a bloody handprint lying on the beach? Not only was it bad news, it was cliched bad news. But for whatever reason he could not stop himself from instead grasping the brass-colored handle on the zipper that closed the bag's main compartment and pulling it open.

The sun illuminated the contents easily, and the breath caught in Harry's throat.

That was a lot of money. It was loose, unbundled, but it looked like mostly 20s and 50s, and it filled the bag most of the way.

What was going on here?

"Hi neighbor!"

Harry jerked upright at the sound of a young female voice, and turned. She stood about five foot five, and had wavy dark-brown hair that hung to just past her shoulders, though this morning it was pulled back into a ponytail. Her bikini was pink with little white flower shapes on it, and she filled it out nicely: the muscles of her abdomen were just barely visible, she had nice hips, and Harry's trained eye placed her in a B-cup, maybe a small C. She had shades on, and had a floral-pattern beach bag thrown over one shoulder. A pair of black-soled flip flops dangled from her left hand.

He recognized her immediately. Stacey, from the rental next door to his. He'd noticed her when she and her friends moved in and they had exchanged hellos, but that was it, though he had made a mental note to follow up with her at the first opportunity.

Stacey grinned at him, a warm and inviting grin that Harry was tempted to imagine was just for him. Of course, he knew better. "Harry, right?"

He wiped his hands off on his swim trunks and straightened fully. "Yeah. Good to see you again,

Stacey." He looked quickly around and, seeing she was alone, added, "Your girlfriends aren't joining you today?"

She shrugged. "They wanted to go shopping."

Harry blinked. "But you didn't?"

"Nope."

A woman who didn't want to go shopping? Harry definitely needed to follow up with her. All of a sudden he was thinking maybe the swim could wait. Maybe he ought to stay on the beach for a while. Or even better, maybe she'd care for a dip is a fresh water pool instead of the salty sea. As soon as he figured out what to do about -

"That's Karen's bag," Stacey said, out of the blue, and Harry blinked in surprise.

"Who's Karen?"

"She's renting the house next to us, on the other side from you." Stacey looked around, frowning. "Where is she?"

Well, that was one mystery solved. Harry glanced over toward the dunes. His house was to the left after the path met up with the road. Stacey and her friends' was directly adjacent to the path on the right. Which meant Karen's was the next one on the right, and just about even with where the bag was lying. Someone could have thrown the bag over the dune. But why get rid of a bag full of money?

Given the bloody handprint, he didn't have a lot of trouble coming up with all sorts of reasons why, come to think on it.

"Um, Stacey," Harry said, "I think she might be in trouble. I just found this here, and, well, look for yourself." He squatted down again and gestured toward the bag.

Stacey, frowning, stepped closer and leaned over to examine the bag more closely. As she did, the sun struck her shades at just the right angle to allow him to see her eyes go wide. Her jaw dropped open. "Is that - ?"

Harry nodded. "I think so." He looked closely at her. "What do you know about Karen?"

Stacey gave a little shake and, pursing her lips, straightened. "Not much. She's an artist, I think. Lives there with her daughter."

"No husband?"

She shook her head. "I don't think so." She cocked her head to the side, looking at him with an odd expression on her face. "Are you a cop or something?"

He snorted and stood back up. "No. Not anymore."

Her eyebrow lifted, and he saw the question there. But she didn't ask it, instead saying, "But you've called them, right?"

"No, like I said I just found the bag." Although, come to think on it… "You said she's an artist. Does she paint?"

"I dunno, I guess. Why - ?" Then she burst out in a little, relieved, laugh. "That could be paint. Red paint!"

Well, blood was not nearly as thick as paint, so Harry sort of doubted it. Maybe watercolor? Still, if it helped Stacey keep calm while they figured this out…and who knows, it could be true. "Could be. I hope so." He bent over and picked up the bag by its carrying handles. "Before we get the cops involved, let's make sure this isn't just us jumping to conclusions." He looked back at Stacey. "Will you come along? You've met her. Might be weird if a stranger showed up with her her bag of money."

She chuckled and nodded briskly. "No kidding."

Harry took a minute to pick up his things and

get all of his burdens more comfortably arranged. Then the two of them turned toward the path leading through the dunes.

As they came out the other side, he nodded toward his place, on the left. "I'm going to drop my stuff off real quick," he said, and she nodded concurrence.

His rental had a grey stone privacy wall between the path and his back yard, just high enough that he could peek over it on tip-toe. It was broken halfway between its commencement just below the dune and the street ahead by a red-stained wooden gate with a simple lifting latch. Not exactly prime security, but it did the job of keeping prying eyes out.

Opening the gate, he flashed Stacey a quick grin then stepped onto his pool deck.

Poured cement, with blue and white fish-shapes inlaid around the perimeter of the pool, the deck area was simple enough to almost be elegant. A trio of yellow and white chaise lounges sat on the dune side of the pool, and a glass-topped table with seating for six and a matching yellow and white umbrella sat off to the right on the house side, near a bricked-in barbecue pit and a granite-topped bar complete with kegorator.

Not a bad place to hang out.

As Harry dropped his bag and chair, leaning the later against the bar, Stacey let out a low whistle.

"Nice pool," she said, appreciatively. "Sure beats what we've got at our place."

Harry shrugged. "It works." He turned back to her and hefted the bag of money. "You ready?"

She looked away from the inviting water toward the bag, and Harry could see the concern in her expression. She nodded.

Stacey led the way back out the gate.

Karen's house was a one-story beige-stucco bungalow set back from the road about thirty feet. In lieu of a driveway, the area immediately off the road was just graveled in, offering space to park three cars. Maybe four, if they squeezed. Right now there were two: a red Honda Civic and a silvery-grey Subaru Outback. A pair of palm trees stood on either side of a little walking path leading from the parking area to her white-painted front door. Long windows on either side of the door offered views into the living areas, but the interior was dark compared with the noonday sun and Harry could not see much detail.

He frowned, considering the cars for a second. "Either of those hers?"

Stacey nodded. "The Outback." She paused, the added, "Don't know about the other one."

Well, Karen was home at least. That was something, and helped rule out foul play. At least, that's what Harry hoped.

They walked up to the front door, and Harry knocked three times. When, after a long ten count, no one came to the door, he looked over at Stacey, who gave a little shrug.

"She's here," she said, and reached out and tried the doorknob.

It turned freely, and the door swung open on silent hinges.

The lights were out in the entryway and the living room beyond, but there was more than enough sunlight to see details. The floor was yellow-brown stone, polished to a dull shine. The furnishings in the living room were spare, no frills. Which probably meant they were pretty darn comfortable. A small wood stove stood in the rear left corner, the black cast iron of its chimney rising through the ceiling in place of a fireplace. Directly opposite the front door, an open archway led to a hallway leading further back into the house. On the rear wall was a large oil painting of the seashore. Windows dominated the left-hand wall, and the wall to the right held framed pictures of a homely blonde woman of about thirty-five with a pre-teen girl who had her same hair, nose, and eyes.

"Karen and daughter, I presume," Harry said to himself. He had not intended the words for Stacey, but she responded with a "Yeah" anyway.

They hesitated in the doorway, watching and listening. The place seemed deserted; there was no sound besides their breathing. If not for the lingering odor of bacon on the air, Harry would have thought no one had been in the house in days.

"Doesn't look like she's here," he said, doubtfully.

Stacey looked left and right again, then took a slow step inside, pushing her shades up onto her forehead. "Karen?" she called. "Are you home?"

A muffled noise, hard to put a name on, came from the back of the house. There was someone here after all.

Harry traded a glance with Stacey then, handing the bag of money to her, took the lead into the hallway. It wasn't exactly narrow, but he would have to turn sideways to let another person pass comfortably down it. More photos of family and friends hung on the walls, and they passed a powder room on the right, then a small bedroom that had been turned into an office on the left. Then the hallway opened into a combination kitchen/dining area that looked like it had been transported from the 60s.

It was all linoleum and garish colors, with old

appliances and a dining room table that appeared to have been painted and re-painted several times from all the streaks of color on it. Off to the right, past the kitchen area, another hallway led, presumably, to the bedrooms, and there was a sliding glass door at the rear leading out into the back yard. Royal blue hanging drapes hanging from casters in the ceiling were mostly drawn across the rear door and the floor-to-ceiling window that took up most of the rest of the back wall, letting sunlight spill into the room.

The sliding glass door was open, and the sea breeze made the drapes billow slightly as it brought the day's heat inside to fight with the air conditioned air within.

As he stepped into the room, it was obvious to Harry that there had been some kind of trouble here. Dining chairs were knocked over, and an empty glass lay on the floor next to one of them, a spreading puddle of water marking its former contents. Two plates, both with bacon and eggs lying half-eaten on them, sat on the table, and dirty pans were on the stove.

"This doesn't look good," Stacey said as she looked around. Then, more loudly, she called out, "Karen!" She waited a second, then turned to look at Harry. "I think we should call the cops now."

Harry was just nodding his head to agree when another noise came from the back yard. It sounded like an impact of some sort, and maybe a voice, but he couldn't make out the words. But the tone was unmistakable: anger, desperation, and malice all rolled into one.

"Make the call," he said, and hurried to the sliding glass door.

The back yard was nothing fancy. A smallish concrete pad where Karen had set up a grill and a little metal-and-plastic table set for two, and the rest was grass going to sand as it approached the dunes in the rear. About halfway back lay a new-looking wooden outbuilding. More than a shed, it was almost the size of the kitchen/dining room in the house, painted grey, and had electrical wires running to it from the corner of the house. It had a set of double doors for an entrance that were closed, but a quick glance around showed nowhere else anyone could be on the property, and privacy fences on either side would have prevented them from going into the neighbors' places.

So the out-building it was.

Harry strode over with the quick, purposeful walk he reserved for when he really meant business…and he thought someone might be watching. Over the years, that walk alone had prompted some tough guys to back down from a fight. Here's hoping a similar result happened this time.

Reaching the double doors, he paused. From inside the out-building he could hear sounds of movement, or things being pushed or thrown around. And something else, almost like a voice but muffled. Then something shattered within and he heard a loud, salty curse.

"Where is it?"

That was the first intelligible words he had heard. They came from a female voice, filled with anger. And near-panic. Whoever that was, she was on the ragged edge. Probably knew she was jail-bound but was past the line with no way to pull back. That kind of person was dangerous.

Time to put a stop to whatever was going on in there. He grasped the doorknobs and pulled the double-doors open.

The inside of the out-building was set up as a studio. Easels and canvases were stacked against the left wall, the ones near the back blank and the ones toward the front splashed with swaths of color of all shades in random patterns, or filled with paintings of people in various poses, and a few landscapes as well. To Harry's untrained eye, the paintings didn't look like anything special.

The right-hand side of the building held pottery and sculpting equipment. There was a potter's wheel and a kiln, an unstained wooden chest of drawers that was topped with a bunch of jars and containers, and resting on a little stand toward the rear a block of what looked like marble, but probably wasn't, that someone had begun carving into. The vague form of a four-legged animal was beginning to take shape, but it was far from done.

The entire place was lit by a pair of fluorescent tracks mounted to the ceiling, and a little wall-mounted air conditioning unit whirred in the back corner.

Harry took all that in at a glance, but what caught and held his attention like a vice was the action in the center of the building. The blonde woman and girl from the picture in the living room of the house were tied hand and foot, gagged, and plopped down next to next other on a threadbare love seat that sat against the middle of the rear wall. Both were in their pajamas, and looked frightened out of their wits. A short, stocky, black-haired fellow in blue jeans and a loose short-sleeved white collared shirt, with sweat stains running down the back from the day's heat, stood looming over them.

A woman, chubby with close-cropped hair that had been died pink and a loop-earring through her left nostril, was rummaging through the chest of drawers. She wore a loose-fitting navy blue blouse that was unbuttoned one button too far and slightly too tight white pants, and her face was a mask of chagrin.

Both of the bad guys spun to face him as he opened the doors, the influx of sunlight giving his presence away immediately. Both jaws dropped in surprise, and both sets of eyes widened in chagrin.

"Well, isn't this special?" Harry said before they could get a word out, and he crossed his arms over his chest. He was painfully aware that he likely appeared less than threatening in his board shorts, tank top, and flip flops, with his shades pushed up onto his forehead. More like a surfer than a savior. But he had a couple inches on the guy, and was in better shape besides. Hopefully these two would be spooked enough about what they were doing to not start anything.

"You guys are in heaps of trouble, you know that?" he continued, keeping his tone as conversational as possible. "The police are on the way, so how about you make nice, untie the lady and her daughter, sit down over there," he jerked his jaw toward a space on the floor between the kiln and the partially completed sculpture, "and be a good little boy and girl until they get here. No need to make this harder than it's going to be."

The woman and the man traded looks. She scowled and jerked her head Harry's way.

Let's you and him fight. Typical. Even odds she had made him do the tying up, too.

The guy didn't look enthused, but he squared his shoulders and took a step in Harry's direction. "You made a big mistake coming here, buddy," he said in a tone that almost but not quite didn't proclaim confidence that he was going to put Harry down.

"That makes three of us then," Harry said, not

moving but putting on what he hoped was a cheerful smile. "Don't make another one."

The guy sniffed and came forward, driving an obvious, slow, and lumbering right fist toward Harry's face.

Harry managed to sigh with disgust as he bobbed to the side out of the punch's way and drove a left upper cut into the guy's liver.

The guy's eyes bugged out and he coughed out an "Ugh!" as he doubled over.

Harry shook his head and considered for a second, the popped him in the side of the jaw with a right. The guy went down onto his left side and stayed there, groaning.

"Moron." Harry looked up from the vanquished man toward Pink-hair. He pointed a commanding finger at her, then at the floor. "Siddown."

Pink-hair's eyes had gone wide as saucers. They were fixed on her fallen white knight, and she was shaking hard. Either she hadn't heard Harry or his words hadn't registered.

He tried again. "Sit. Down. Now," he said again, putting a biting command into each word.

She sat.

Behind him, he heard footsteps through grass, then Stacey's voice. "Nice work," she said as he came up next to him. She eyed the fallen man appreciatively, then turned to grin at Harry after a second. It was the kind of look that would have sent butterflies through his belly back when he was thirteen. Today they made him grin inwardly, in anticipation.

"Why don't you untie them? I'll watch these two."

Stacey bobbed a nod, then set to it.

The police arrived fifteen minutes later, and

they set to the taking of statements and booking the bad guys.

Turns out Pink-hair was Karen's manager. Agent. Whatever they called it. She had been hounding Karen for weeks, claiming Karen owed her money for an exhibition she had booked a month ago, which of course Karen denied. When Karen showed up with Chad—of course they White Knight's name was Chad—demanding the money, Karen had sent her daughter to hide the bag while she dealt with them. The daughter had heard the growing altercation and panicked, knocking over a can of red paint in her haste to find a hiding spot. In the end she had thrown the bag up onto the dune, and then ran back to try to help. She had thrown the bag harder than she thought, because it made it over the dune entirely.

Chad was good at forcing women into submission, if nothing else. He had tied and gagged them while Pink-hair searched around, and that's when Harry walked in.

It didn't seem like they had much of a plan beyond that. But then, those types never did, did they? Even money Pink Hair had a legit complaint. Harry wouldn't have been surprised to learn Karen had been stiffing her for a long time. Not that it mattered now. Morons.

Two hours later, the cops were gone with the perps, and Karen and her daughter had followed in their own car to finish giving their statements at the station.

Harry and Stacey watched the little caravan pull off down the road from the front of Karen's house, and Harry couldn't help but feel quite satisfied with himself. He'd saved the day and it wasn't even three o'clock. Not a bad bit of work, if he did say so himself.

"All's well that ends well, eh?" He turned to look fully at Stacey, and put on his best, most inviting smile. "I don't know about you, but I think this calls for a celebration."

She returned his look gamely, arching one eyebrow. "Oh yeah?" She moved a couple inches closer, looking up at his face with the smallest of secretive smiles. "What did you have in mind?"

"I was thinking of grilling up a burger, having a beer, and taking a dip in the pool." He let that sink in for a second. "You game?"

That little smile grew to a warm, almost sultry grin. "Sounds good."

Yeah, a pretty good day's work. And it was looking like the rest of the day was going to be even better.

Thank you for reading my book. I hope you enjoyed reading it as much as I enjoyed writing it.

Every review helps an author out, so whether you loved this book, hated it, or something in between, please take a minute to tell other readers what you thought. All of the online retailers make it very easy to do, and I would really appreciate it.

Feel free to come say hi at my website or on Facebook. I always enjoy hearing from readers, especially since you all are, collectively, my boss.

I also have a weekly podcast, Story Time With Michael Kingswood, where I read stories and talk through some of the latest goings on in my world. I'd love to see you there.

Thanks again. My best to you and yours.

Warm Regards,
Michael Kingswood

Mailing List

If you enjoyed this book and would like word on new releases and special deals from Michael Kingswood, sign up for his newsletter on his website. Guaranteed to be spam-free, you can opt out at any time. And you can rest assured he will not share your information with anyone, for any reason.

https://michaelkingswood.com/newsletter-signup/

About The Author

Michael Kingswood is 20-year veteran of the US Navy submarine force and a lifelong fan of science fiction and fantasy literature. His work has appeared in numerous collections and anthologies, to include the Fiction River Anthology series from WMG publishing. He holds a bachelors degree in Mechanical Engineering as well as a Master of Engineering Management and a Master of Business Administration. He has four children and currently resides in San Diego.

Find Michael Kingswood online at:

www.michaelkingswood.com

www.facebook.com/michael.kingswood

steemit.com/@michaelkingswood

More Books By Michael Kingswood

Glimmer Vale Chronicles

Glimmer Vale

Out-Dweller

Tollard's Peak

Robbed Blind

Wedding Gifts: A Glimmer Vale Chronicles Story

The Falconer's Stairs

Glimmer Vale Omnibus Edition #1

The Pericles Conspiracy

Passing In The Night

The Pericles Conspiracy

Dawn Of Enlightenment

Masters Of The Sun

Novellas

What Lurks Between

The Necromancer's Lair

The Champion
Veritas Morte

Story Collections

Tales Of Adventure #1
Tales Of Adventure #2
Short Story 10-Pack
A Jar Of Mixed Treats
Short Mystery 10-Pack

Short Fiction

Michael has also published a number of shorter works,
links to which can be found on his website.

www.ingramcontent.com/pod-product-compliance
Lightning Source LLC
Chambersburg PA
CBHW032054180726
48284CB00004B/1334